Santa's Hat

Written by Nancy Claus

Illustrated by Steve Ferchaud

Cypress Bay Publishing • Woodbridge, CA.
www.cypressbaypublishing.com

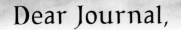

Dear Journal,

It is Christmas Eve day and there is so much excitement coming from Santa's workshop. All the last minute toys are being made. Santa is checking his list. The elves are busy loading Santa's sleigh. And the reindeer, well the reindeer are doing what they do best; eating their favorite snacks.

Children are always asking why their parents are so rushed at Christmas, shopping, wrapping, and decorating They say there's not enough time to get everything done, and yet kids feel like Christmas will never get here.

I'll tell you a little secret.
Sometimes Santa has to slow
down time, so he can see everyone.
So when you're feeling like you
can't wait any longer, you are feeling
Santa's magical time.

I'd better close.
Teagan and I are off to the stocking room.
Would you like to come?

Look at the piles of toys. It looks like Gregory
and Kimberly are busy organizing everything.
"Could we help?"
"Oh hi Mrs. Claus!"
"Hi Teagan."
"We're ahead of schedule this year. Santa gave us paper
bags with all the kids' names on them. We're filling the
bags so Santa will be able to go faster when he's filling
their stockings. I just hope we'll be able to fit all the bags
on his sleigh."

"What a great idea. Don't worry I'm sure
everything will fit.
If you don't need us, we're off to the
toy room."

"Wow! Look at how many toys are on the way to Santa's sleigh.
It looks like Toby has everything under control.
He has plenty of help."

"We're not needed here, so lets go to the kitchen."

"Mrs. Claus we've been looking everywhere for you. We started baking our pies for Christmas day dinner. We took them out of the oven to let them cool. Then instead of us having a feast, our new baby reindeer are having a feast, and what a mess they made. We'll never have dinner ready in time."

"Sure we will. I'll get some help.
We'll work together as a team.
Start cleaning and I'll be right back."

"I can't find my hat, have you seen it?"
"Yes, I left it on your chair."
"It's not there."
"Uh, Oh! Sparkle and Simone were asking me earlier if they could try on your hat?"
"I told them they would have to ask you."
"I haven't seen either one of them all day."

"Let's use the loud speaker to ask."

"Attention all Elves! Has anyone seen Santa's hat?
It's time for him to leave. Oh Yes; Sparkle and
Simone I need to see both of you right away."

"Did you hear your name?"
"I think so. Did you hear yours?"
"I think we might be in big trouble.
 We better put Santa's hat back."

"Watch the milk, Sparkle!"
"Oh no! Santa's hat slipped
and fell into the milk.
What shall we do?"
"I think we better go find
Mrs.Claus right away."

"Sparkle, have you seen Santa's
  hat?"
"Umm, we had a little accident."
"What kind of accident?"
"We dropped Santa's hat in spilled
  milk."
"Oh my, Santa needs his hat. Let
  me think for a moment."

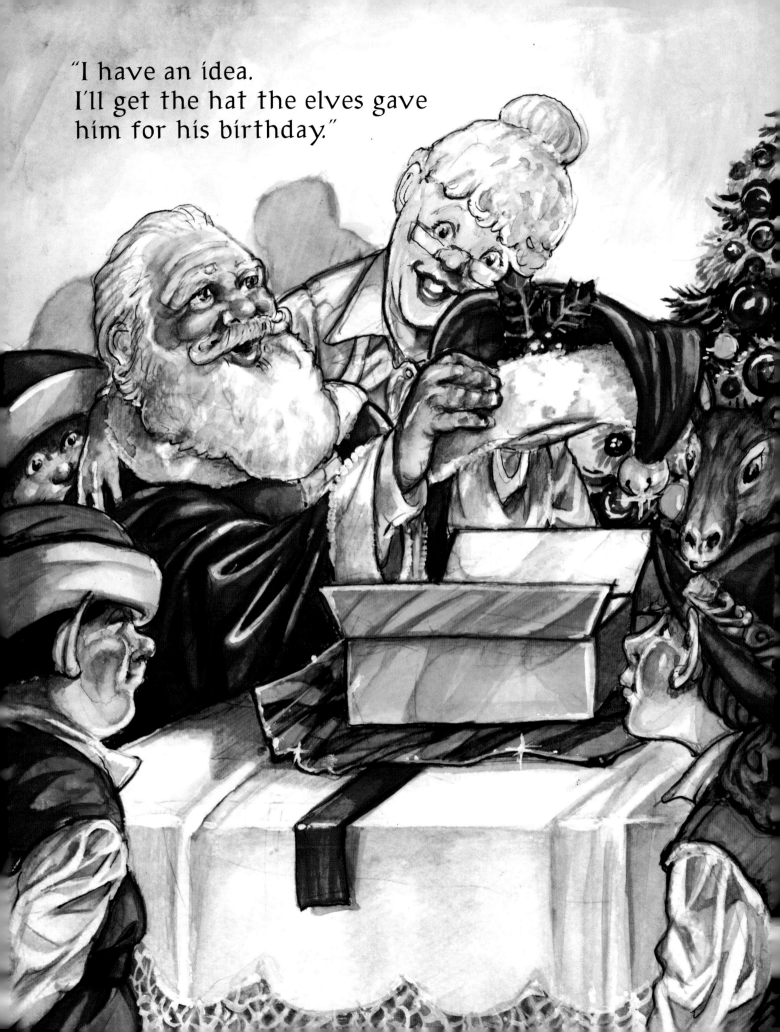

"I have an idea.
I'll get the hat the elves gave
him for his birthday."

"Santa, try on your new hat."
"Oh my, Santa you do look handsome."
"Thank you. I better go now."
"Have a good trip, Santa."
"Ok, I'll be back for more toys when my sleigh is empty. I love you!"
"I love you too, Santa. Be careful."

"Toby, are the toys tied down?"
"Yes, Santa, and all your stockings are in the back
 of your sleigh."
"How about the reindeer, Dasher, Dancer, Prancer
 and Vixen, Comet, Cupid, Donner, and Blitzen?

Finally they flew off into the night.

I hope you don't think that's the end of the story.
Remember the mess?
Follow me to the kitchen to see how I can help.

"What! I don't believe my eyes. Not only is the kitchen clean, but the pies are all made as well. Sparkle, who did all this?"

"We did, Simone and I. Our dad helped us. We had to hurry so he wouldn't be late for Santa. We're so lucky our dad is Rudolph. He told us we had to be more careful when we play, and not to expect anyone else to clean up our mess."

"We're sorry, Mrs. Claus. We've learned our lesson. It was just so hard when Boots the Baker made all those good smells come from the kitchen."
"I know. Sometimes I want to taste everything as it comes out of the oven, too. Thank you for cleaning it all up."

The rest of the day went well. Santa came back a few times to reload his sleigh. He said his new hat was keeping his ears nice and warm.

It wasn't until Christmas Day that we had our feast. It was worth the wait.

The best part of our feast is listening to Santa's stories about his flight.
Someday I'll tell you about it. But for now I hope everyone has a happy Christmas.
I'm looking forward to a nice nap.

Love,
Mrs.Claus

To my Grandchildren:
You inspire, you bring laughter, you make my heart sing.
Love, Nana

Santa's Hat written by Nancy Claus
Copyright ©2006 Nancy Claus

Published by Cypress Bay Publishing
P.O. Box 984
Woodbridge, CA 95258-0984
www.cypressbaypublishing.com

Text&Story Copyright ©2006 by Nancy Claus
Illustrations Copyright ©2006 Steve Ferchaud
Cover Design - Steve Ferchaud and Tom Watson
Layout and Design editors - Book Builders.net
Senior Editor - Rene Schmidt
Publisher - Cypress Bay Publishing

"Santa's Hat" ISBN 978-0-9746747-6-6
Library of Congress Control Number (LCC) 2006902416
BISAC: JUV017010 Juvenile Fiction/Holidays & Celebrations/Christmas

Summary - Mrs. Claus tells how Santa gets ready for his busy Christmas Eve flight.

Additional subjects: Santa Claus, Mrs. Claus, Elves, Holidays, Celebrations, Christmas Eve

Printed In Hong Kong   First Edition   First Printing